You Can Make a Friend, Pout-Pout Fish!

Deborah Diesen

Pictures by Isidre Monés, based on illustrations
created by Dan Hanna for the *New York Times*—
bestselling Pout-Pout Fish books

Farrar Straus Giroux
New York

Farrar Straus Giroux Books for Young Readers
An imprint of Macmillan Publishing Group, LLC
175 Fifth Avenue, New York, NY 10010

Color separations by Embassy Graphics
Printed in China by RR Donnelley Asia Printing Solutions Ltd., Dongguan City, Guangdong Province
Designed by Roberta Pressel
First edition, 2018
Hardcover: 1 3 5 7 9 10 8 6 4 2
Paperback: 1 3 5 7 9 10 8 6 4 2

mackids.com

Library of Congress Control Number: 2017956503

Hardcover ISBN: 978-0-374-30982-4
Paperback ISBN: 978-1-250-06428-8

Our books may be purchased in bulk for promotional, educational, or business use.
Please contact your local bookseller or the Macmillan Corporate and Premium Sales Department
at (800) 221-7945 ext. 5442 or by e-mail at MacmillanSpecialMarkets@macmillan.com.

Mr. Fish was about to pout.
He did not have a friend at school.

He did not have a friend
to talk to.

He did not have a friend to sit by.

He did not have a friend
to play with.

Bluuuuuuuuuuuub!

"What can I do?" said Mr. Fish.

"How do I make a friend?"

He thought.
He looked around.
He thought some more.
Then he had an idea.

His idea was to try!
Maybe it would not be
so hard.

Mr. Fish smiled.

He swam forward.

"Hello," said Mr. Fish.

"Hi!" said Ms. Clam.

"Sit with us," said Mr. Fish.

"Thank you!" said Mr. Crab.

"Join us," said Mr. Fish.

"I will!" said Mrs. Squid.

Mr. Fish had a good day.
His class had a good day.
They all had fun!

"I like school," said Mr. Fish.
He did not have a friend at
school . . .

. . . he had *three* friends!

And more to come!

"I can make friends at school," said Mr. Fish.

"No pout about it!"